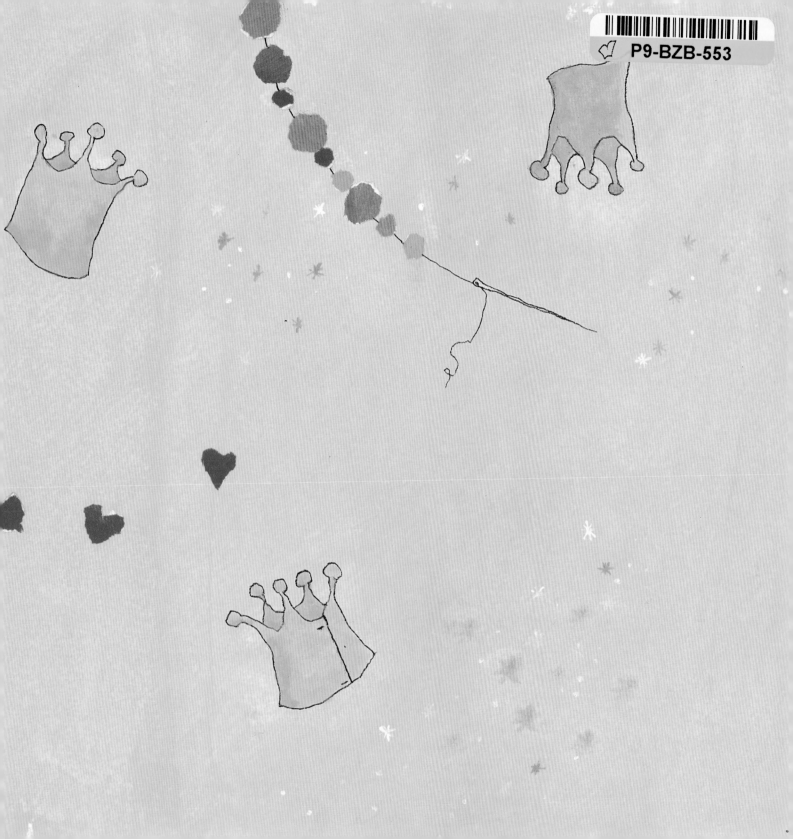

For all the princesses of the world

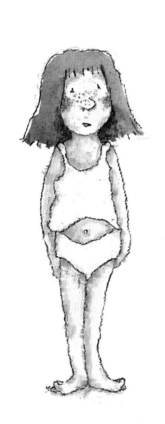

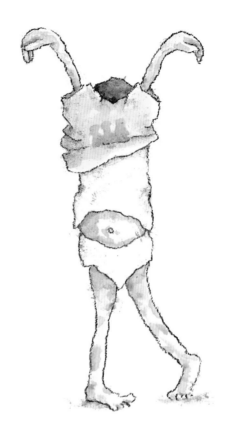

First American Edition 2001 by Kane/Miller Book Publishers
La Jolla, California

First published in the Netherlands in 1999 under the title En dan was ik de prinses by Van Goor/De Boekerij bv, Amsterdam

Copyright ° 1999 Van Goor/De Boekerij bv, Amsterdam
American Text copyright 2001 Kane/Miller Book Publishers

Library of Congress Catalog Card Number 2001089880

Printed and bound in Singapore

1 2 3 4 5 6 7 8 9 10

Tiny Fisscher
The Four Princesses

Illustrated By
Barbara de Wolf

Kane/Miller
BOOK PUBLISHERS

I'm a princess.

But I still look like an ordinary girl.

Now do I look more like
a princess?

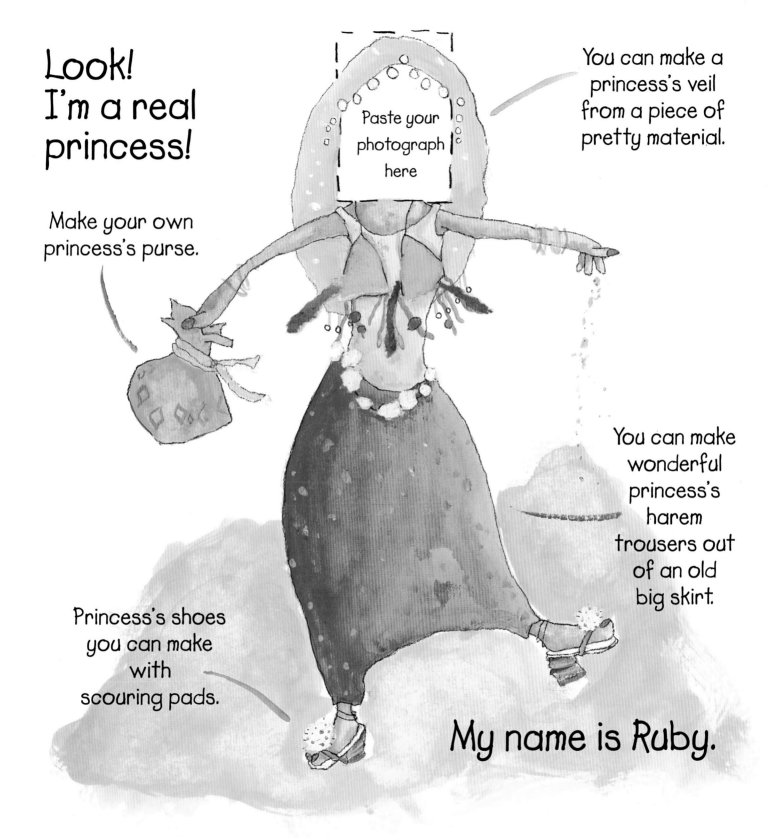

Look!
I'm a real
princess!

You can make a
princess's veil
from a piece of
pretty material.

Paste your
photograph
here

Make your own
princess's purse.

You can make
wonderful
princess's
harem
trousers out
of an old
big skirt.

Princess's shoes
you can make
with
scouring pads.

My name is Ruby.

Ruby's veil

What you need:
★ wide headband
★ scarf
★ long imitation pearl necklace, tinsel or ribbon
★ scissors
★ tape
★ piece of ribbon
8 inches long

Tape the short side of the scarf to the underside of the headband. Wrap the scarf once around the headband. Now the scarf will fall over your hair and down your back. If you cut the scarf in the middle about 6 inches from the bottom, then you can drape the two halves over your shoulders.

Find the middle of the necklace and tie it to the headband with the ribbon. Put the headband and the scarf on your head and place the necklace, which will fall down over your face, behind your ears. Now you look as though you're wearing very long elegant earrings (see picture).

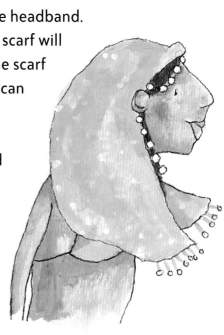

Ruby's shoes

What you need:
★ flip-flops ★ 6 colored scouring pads
★ two cotton balls
★ glue ★ glitter

Glue three scouring pads together, with the rough side up each time.
Let them dry, and then glue them to the underside of the flip-flops to make a heel (see picture).
Sprinkle glitter onto the cotton balls and glue one to each shoe.

Ruby's top

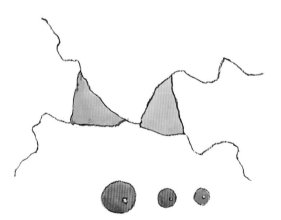

What you need:
★ bikini top
★ twelve pieces of ribbon
(from 2 to 6 inches long)
★ leotard or bathing suit
★ large beads

Put on the leotard or bathing suit. Tie the ribbons onto the underside of the bikini top (see picture) and put it on. You can thread a bead onto each ribbon. Make a knot at the end of the ribbon, otherwise the bead will fall off. If the bikini doesn't have string to tie the ribbons to, then you can use tape to stick the ribbons to the inside of the bikini top.

Ruby's harem trousers

What you need:
★ a grown-up's old skirt
★ two ribbons or strips of material
★ a belt

Put on the skirt and fasten it at the waist with the belt.
Fasten the skirt at both knees with a ribbon.
This will make the skirt puff out at the knees, making
a perfect pair of oriental harem trousers.

Ruby's handbag

What you need:
★ a marble bag/shoe bag or else a
square of material about 8 inches by 8 inches
★ beads, buttons, dried beans or uncooked macaroni
★ a piece of ribbon

Fill the marble bag/shoe bag with the beads, buttons, dried beans or uncooked
macaroni and then tie it up with the piece of ribbon. Or put the beads, buttons,
and other filling onto the middle of the piece of material. You can make this into
a bag by gathering up the corners and then tying them together with the ribbon.

Finishing Touches

To complete your princess's outfit, you can stick a little red paper circle in the middle of your forehead. You can also make a little circle with lipstick or greasepaint.

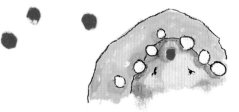

Princess Ruby's customs

Oriental princesses sit or lie on lots of cushions on the ground.
They drink tea out of pretty teacups and eat Turkish delight or raisins.

Ruby

In a warm, dry, sandy land, far, far away, a Sultan lived with his wife and four daughters in a fabulous castle made of sand. The Sultan was short and fat with an enormous nose, thin, spiky hair and stumpy legs. He found this most unfair. After all, a Sultan was supposed to look strong and powerful. That's why he would never leave the castle without a mountainous turban on his head and high platform shoes on his feet. He also stuffed lots of padding under his coat so he would look strong and tough. When he spoke, he tried to make his voice sound like thunder and he hardly ever laughed. Sultans definitely don't laugh, he decided. As well as all this he was horribly stingy. On the first day of every month he would have all the grains of sand in his kingdom carefully counted just to make sure they were still there.

"And you're not allowed to play with the sand!" he always screamed at the children. "That's not what it's for!"

The Sultan's wife was quite different. She was tall and rather thin. She couldn't really care less about all that sand. She would giggle, and chuckle, and burst out laughing – all at the drop of a hat, much to the annoyance of the Sultan.

"Stop that childish sniggering!" he would thunder. But his wife would always giggle for just a couple of seconds longer, because she could never stop straightaway.

Three of the Sultan's daughters were the same age and looked exactly alike. As a matter of fact, they were triplets, and each had her own tower. Their names were Millicent, Mildred and Minerva and they were always together. As nobody could tell which was which, not even their own father and mother, they were just called Mi, Mi and Mi. This was particularly convenient when they had to be sent for. Then you could hear "Mimimi!" all over the castle.

When the three Princesses were nearly grown up, a new little sister arrived quite unexpectedly. The Sultan was most displeased. "That means I'll have to order another tower to be built," he grumbled. In fact, he was afraid that it would be triplets all over again and that would mean having three more towers built.

The new little Princess (there turned out to be just one after all) was named Ruby, because she had red hair and she was very beautiful. "Isn't she precious?" her mother said. And besides, with a name like Ruby, she would never get confused with her three sisters.

When Ruby was four years old she was allowed to go outside for the first time. She rode in a golden carriage, high up on top of Casper, the castle camel.
The Princess couldn't believe her eyes.
"What a lot of sand," she cried.
"Yes, and it's all mine!" said the Sultan, smiling proudly.
"I've got so much sand you can't even see where my country ends. My country goes on forever!"
Ruby was dumbfounded. Sand, sand and more sand – even the houses were made of sand.

As they got further away from the castle, Ruby saw people who lived under roofs made of cloth.

"Don't those people have houses?" she asked in surprise.

"No," her father answered, as if this was perfectly normal.

"Why not?"

"Because they have no money to buy sand."

Ruby looked across the vast sand plain.

"Oh..."

The years passed by. Ruby grew up into a beautiful girl with fiery red hair and shining brown eyes.

Her three sisters, in the meantime, no longer lived in the castle. They were married to John, James and Jerome, three rather dull prince triplets from another sandy country not too far away.

Yuck, thought Ruby, just imagine having to marry a prince like that. I'd never do that, she thought. She would have liked to visit her sisters, though, but her father wouldn't let her. After that one trip on Casper she had never been outside the castle walls.

"Why don't we ever go out?" Ruby would ask.

"Because you're too curious!" her father would shout. "That's dangerous!"

Ruby simply could not understand this. One day she thought, If daddy won't allow me outside the castle, then I'll sneak out!

Very early the next morning she crept past the snoring guards and out of the castle gate.

She looked around wide-eyed. She saw men pushing carts, women with baskets on their heads and donkeys with bags on their backs. And she still saw people without houses.

How terrible! she thought. How can Papa approve?

The next day Ruby found a flower behind her door, together with a little note.

"Are you coming out to play?" it said. Nothing else.

Ruby went red with excitement. Nothing like this had ever happened to her.

However did that note get there? She quickly hid it and went down-stairs to breakfast.

"Hello mum, hello dad!" she cried merrily.

"Mmm," her father mumbled grumpily.

"Good morning darling!" her mother giggled. "Boiled egg?"

The Sultan's wife missed her other three daughters terribly and each day she hoped for a letter.

"Hooray, the mail!" she shrieked in delight, as soon as she heard the clatter of the mail-box. She ran to the door and was back in a flash, waving a letter.

"Look what I've got!" Impatiently she tore open the letter.

"Tee, hee, hee! Twelve! Tee, hee, hee!"

She dropped the letter, ran outside roaring with laughter, and rushed towards Casper the camel.

"What's going on now?" thundered the Sultan. Ruby picked up the letter.

"Mum," she read out loud. "We've just had twelve babies and we can't keep them quiet. Come quickly. Mi, Mi and Mi."

The Sultan clasped his hands to his head.

"Twelve! Oh no! I'll have go on a trip to buy new sand for twelve new towers!"

And out he ran, without even saying goodbye.

"Dad," Ruby called out after him. But her father didn't hear.

The Princess sighed. Dad gone, Mum gone, Casper gone. I'm going too, she thought. And she walked out of the castle gate, cool as can be.

The Princess walked through the village, past all the houses and past the people without houses.

I wish I could build castles for all of them, she thought.

She knelt down and buried her hands in the warm sand.

She made a little pile, but it just fell in.

She tried again, but again it fell.

"Are you playing?" asked a soft voice.

The little Princess looked up in surprise and saw a boy with a laughing face and two merry dimples in his cheeks.

"No, I want to build a sandcastle, but it keeps falling in. Can you help me?"

"But surely your father won't allow that!" the boy said, shocked.

"How do you know who my father is?"

"I s-saw you w-wandering around yesterday m-morning," the boy stammered.

"Did you write that letter?"

The boy nodded shyly.

"I crept inside the palace," he whispered.

"That was brave of you!" Ruby took his hand. "Come on, let's build a sandcastle. Anyhow, my father's not here."

The boy hesitated.

"Please?" Ruby begged.

Reluctantly the boy took her to a well. There he showed Ruby how to use water to make the sand stay together.

"Oh, how clever!" cried Ruby.

"You can do it too," the boy said.

A little girl stood watching them, her eyes wide with astonishment. After a while she walked hesitantly over to Ruby and tapped her gently on the shoulder.

Ruby turned around in surprise.

"May I live in that castle when it's ready?" the little girl whispered shyly.

"Of course!" said Ruby.

"Do you want to help us fin...?"

"What's going on here?" a voice thundered.

There was the Sultan, with his guards and a whole herd of camels. Ruby shrank back.

"I … I thought you'd gone out," she stuttered.

"Quite beside the point!" the Sultan boomed.

"How dare you mess around with my sand!
What's this monstrous piece of work?"
He pointed at the sandcastle in disgust.

"I built that," the boy said quickly.

"And I helped…" Ruby chipped in bravely.

"And I'm going to live in it," whispered the little girl.

The Sultan went quite pale. "How dare you!"
He clenched his fists and stomped about in the sand.

"Guards, take them away!"

The Sultan flapped his arms up and down wildly, so wildly that his coat burst open and all the padding flew up into the air. The guards started to giggle nervously.

"Do as I say!" the Sultan shrieked.

The guards turned red in the face, bit their lips and rocked backwards and forwards, clutching their stomachs.

"Don't just stand there like a pack of idiots!" the Sultan yelled in desperation. Furiously he stamped his feet again in the sand.

Just at that moment his platform shoes split in two, and to make matters worse, his turban fell off his head! The guards couldn't contain themselves any longer and burst out laughing.

"Dash, darn and blow!" roared the Sultan. He grabbed at his turban and tried to keep his balance on his broken shoes. But it was too late. Everyone had seen the Sultan for what he really was: a silly, mean little man.

"Ha, ha, and he calls himself Sultan!" cried one of the guards. Everybody doubled up with laughter. Even the camels' knees wobbled with laughter.

"Oh dash it and darn it all!" the Sultan wailed. He buried his head in the sand, so he didn't have to listen to all the laughter. Shrieking with mirth, the guards left for the village, where the story spread like wildfire.

The Princess, the little girl and the boy stood there in dismay.

The Sultan looked so helpless with his head in the sand.

"Oh, poor thing..." the little girl whispered.

Ruby went over to her father and helped him up.

Clumsily, the Sultan wiped the sand off his face.

"Dash it all," he said, giving a little sob.

"Mister Sultan?" asked the little girl, pulling at his trouser leg, "Do you want to play with me?"

"Do you know who I am?" said the Sultan sulkily.

"Cooee!" they heard suddenly. There was Casper jogging along towards them, one laughing granny, three chattering Mi-mummies and twelve bawling babies all piled up on top of his back. Three weary-looking princes rode up behind.

"My poor little Sultan, what a sight you are," his wife giggled. "Now you can't go around looking like that, can you?"

Firmly she picked up his turban from the sand and helped him put it back on.

"There we are, all ready," she said.

Shamefaced, the Sultan just stood where he was.

"My shoes are broken," he sulked.

"Dad," sighed Ruby, "Stop fussing.

Come help us finish this castle."

"Ooh, can we help too?" the Mi-sisters chorused.

The three princes looked gloomily at one another, and sighed, "Shall we just get on with some governing then?"

"No," the Sultan finally said to Ruby. "Finish it yourself."

But for the first time he let the children play with the sand.

Not wholeheartedly, because that was something he still had to learn. And he couldn't resist secretly making sure no-one put any of it into their pocket. For, after all, it did still belong to him.

Make your own princess's hat with stiff paper.

Paste your photograph here

You can make real princess's cuffs with paper cups.

Make a pretty bodice with ribbons.

Decorate your skirt with ribbons.

You can also stamp designs on your skirt.

My name is Rosalie.

Rosalie's party dress

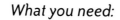

What you need:
- ★ a green t-shirt with long sleeves
- ★ two white paper cups
- ★ about 4 yards of thin white elastic or ribbon
- ★ a long pink skirt or sheet
- ★ a white belt or ribbon ★ scissors ★ safety pins

What you can also use:
- ★ stickers ★ a knife
- ★ two potatoes
- ★ paint, cushions, a large piece of velvet

Put on the t-shirt and the tights.

Cut out the bottom of the paper cups. Put your hand through the narrow end and you'll have a perfect princess's wide cuff. You can decorate the cuffs with stickers.

Don't wrap the elastic or the ribbon around you just yet. Ask a grown-up to wrap it a few times around the top part of your body. Starting from the top it should be crossed over several times and then the elastic or ribbon should be fastened at the back. Make sure it isn't too tight. When it has been crossed two or three times the ends can be fastened together at the back.

Put on the skirt or wrap the sheet around you. Fasten it at the waist so that it doesn't fall down.

If you're allowed to, you can decorate the skirt by cutting out little hearts. With the help of a grown-up, you can cut out a design in a potato, dip it in paint, and make stamps on the skirt. Let the paint dry before you put the skirt on. You can also pin a scarf or a piece of material around the skirt with safety pins. If you put a cushion underneath the skirt at the back (see picture), then you'll look like a real fairytale princess.

As a finishing touch, you can make a cape from a large piece of velvet. Throw it around your shoulders and fasten it at the front with a safety pin or a clothes pin. Ask an adult to help you.

Rosalie's hat

What you need:
★ a sheet of stiff pink paper
16 inches by 8 inches
★ stapler ★ tape ★ scissors
★ three strips of material 4 inches by 8 inches
★ paint or stickers

Take the paper and roll it into a cone (see picture). Stick the edges together with tape. Put the pointed hat on your head, and mark where your ears touch the hat. Attach the strips of material with staples to both sides where you have marked it, so that you can fasten the hat under your chin. Decorate the hat with paint or with stickers. Stick the last strip of material to the top of the hat with tape.

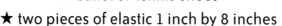

Rosalie's shoes

What you need:
★ ballet or tennis shoes
★ two pieces of elastic 1 inch by 8 inches
★ stapler
★ two pieces of colored or painted
cardboard 6 inches by 6 inches
★ tape

Bend the sides of the cardboard together (see picture). Stick them on the inside with tape. Make it a bit flexible so that you can insert your ballet or tennis shoe into it.

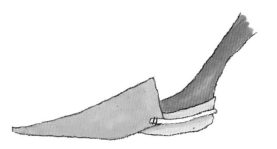

Put your ballet or tennis shoes on and push them gently into the cardboard. Fasten the elastic to one side of the cardboard with staples. Pull the elastic around the back of your heel and remember how long the elastic needs to be so that the shoe fits comfortably. Now fasten the elastic to the other side with staples. Cut off any left-over bits of elastic.

Princess Rosalie's customs

When princesses like Rosalie greet someone, they curtsy.
At the same time they raise their skirt a little.

Princesses like Rosalie love dancing, especially if they
can whirl around with a group in a circle hand in hand.

Rosalie

Once upon a time there was a princess who thought she was so ugly she didn't dare look in the mirror. This was rather odd, because she was really very pretty.

Her hair was like a halo of golden rays around her face. She had clear greeny-blue eyes and a funny little up-turned nose. Even her name was pretty…Rosalie. So why did the Princess think she was so ugly? Well, it's a long story…

When Rosalie was very small, her mother died. The King, who had loved his Queen dearly, was nearly beside himself with grief. For weeks on end he didn't sleep, he didn't eat and he didn't speak. All he did was weep. The only time he felt a little less sad was when he looked at Rosalie, because she looked so much like her mother.

One day Rosalie sighed and said,
"Dad, you're awfully sweet, but life is very empty without a mum around."
The King gulped. But his daughter's happiness came first, so straight-away he put an advertisement in the paper.

Wanted urgently: Mother for princess. Please respond via post to: The King, The Castle, Capital City.

In no time at all, the King got hundreds of letters. Most of them were dull and dreary.

But then a gold-colored envelope caught his eye. The King opened it up and was immediately enchanted by the sweet sounding words. He wrote back: *You sound like the very thing. Come as soon as you can. Greetings from the King.* The woman who had written the letter arrived that same afternoon, and was so beautiful the King nearly fell off his throne. Her delicate face was framed by glossy black hair and she had bewitching deep blue eyes. She had a sweet smile and made funny jokes.

"Will this mum do?" the King asked his daughter.
Rosalie didn't need asking twice. She jumped into her new mum's arms and felt like the luckiest princess in the whole world.

Shortly after their wedding the King invited his new wife for a cup of tea in the summer house. As he opened the door, he cried out proudly, "Allow me to introduce you to the royal parrot!"
But before they'd even got past the doorstep the parrot squawked,
"Ugly witch!"

The Queen went quite red in the face and started to fidget with her gown. "Shame on you, how you dare say such a thing!" the King said in dismay.
"Cup of tea, darling?" asked the Queen,
as if she hadn't heard a thing. "Sugar, milk?"
She made a loud clatter with the spoon as she stirred the tea.
"I say, what a charming room this is," she rattled on.
"So lovely and sunny and the garden is as pretty as a picture, don't you think? Will you please pick me some flowers, darling?"

Straightaway the King did as she asked.
As soon as the Queen was alone with the parrot she hissed at him, "How dare you call me a witch! This is outrageous! Just you keep quiet!"

"Most certainly not! Once a witch, always a witch!" screeched the parrot. "I happen to know who you are!"

The Queen promptly choked. Spluttering with rage, she listened as the parrot went on. "You wanted to marry the King! But you were too ugly for that, weren't you?"

"Ugly! How dare you!" screamed the Queen.

"Yes, ugly! I know jolly well you've been using magic. I bet you've been eating slushy toadstool soup and drinking cockroach juice. And then, of course, you'll have rubbed yourself with snail slime! How did that spell go again?" the parrot taunted her. The Queen fell for the parrot's trick.

"Mumbo-jumbo-creepy-jeeps," she answered without thinking. "Mumbo-jumbo-slikky-slush! Wibble-wobble, crawl right in, wriggle into queenie's skin! Yes, that's the one. That's how I became a beautiful queen! And I'll make sure you don't tell anybody! Ha, I'll cast a spell so you lose your voice!"

Which she promptly did. But nothing happened.

"Ugly witch!" screeched the parrot.

The Queen's eyes blazed with fury. Why wouldn't the spell work? "I'm going to make you disappear!" she cried. She tried another spell, but the parrot just stayed where he was.

"What's going on here?" the queen sputtered. "I'll turn you into a beetle then!"

"It won't work, so there!" cried the parrot.

He was right. However hard the witch tried, she couldn't turn him into a beetle. Nor an ant, nor a centipede.

Soon the King returned, with his arms full of flowers.

At once the parrot called out, "King, watch out! She's an ugly witch!"

"Now, now, parrot dear, what's come over you?" asked the King, quite upset.

"Darling, I think being shut up in a castle has made him lose his little mind. Wouldn't it be better to let him go?" said the Queen.

The King looked shocked.

"Of course not! He was given to us by a good fairy when Rosalie was born! He's a very special bird…"

Well, I'll be dashed! A present from a fairy! That's why I couldn't put a spell on him, thought the Queen angrily. We can't have that!

The next morning the Queen crept out to her witch's hut in the woods and made a secret brew.

"Ah-choo!" the King sneezed, soon after she arrived home.

"Ah-choo!" Rosalie sneezed, and then the footman: "Ah-choo!"

Still sniffling, the King took out his handkerchief. "What's going on here?"

"Ah-choo! I think we've all got parrot allergy,"
the Queen said quickly.

"But he's been living here for ten years!" cried the King.

"And - ah-choo!- he's never made me sneeze before!"

The Queen sighed. "Hmm, ten years, that's just when parrot allergy starts.
What a pity, he'll really have to go."

"No, Dad, - ah-choo! - he can't go," Rosalie begged.

But everyone got so sick of all the sneezing that the King had to do something.
He ordered the footman to shut the parrot in the farthest room in the castle, with
two dishes for food and water.

"Ugly witch!" the parrot kept squawking. But no one heard him with all that sneezing. And even if they had, no one would have believed him. After he was shut away, the Queen quickly cast a spell so that for several weeks no one would think about the poor parrot.

Although the King found his new Queen very beautiful, it was Rosalie who he loved the best.

Well, dash it, we're not having that, thought the jealous Queen.

One day, when she was alone with the Princess, she said, with feigned surprise, "I say, isn't your nose crooked. And what a pathetic little mouth you've got."

The Princess was horrified. "Daddy says that I'm the most beautiful girl in the world!"

"Dear child, that's what fathers always say. But believe me, you really are a most ugly girl. You're very unlucky, aren't you?"

You could have knocked Rosalie over with a feather.

"Come here and let me comb that hair of yours, it's such a mess."

The Queen sat Rosalie down at the dressing table and looked at her in the mirror. "Goodness me, I do believe you're cross-eyed. And how did you get that puny little chin?"

She twisted Rosalie's hair into two straggly braids.

"Poor child, it's just too sad. There's nothing to be done. No wonder nobody loves you."

Rosalie couldn't believe her ears. She was flabbergasted.

"Look at me, dear child," the Queen softly commanded her.

Rosalie looked at her stepmother in the mirror, and the Queen's eyes suddenly started to shine strangely. The Princess felt very sleepy. As if in a dream she heard:

> "You'll tell no one what I'm about to say
> One day, quite soon, you'll go away
> No-one loves you like before
> The King now loves his Queen much more.
> Ugly, ugly Rosalie,
> Now you're bewitched,
> tee-hee-hee!"

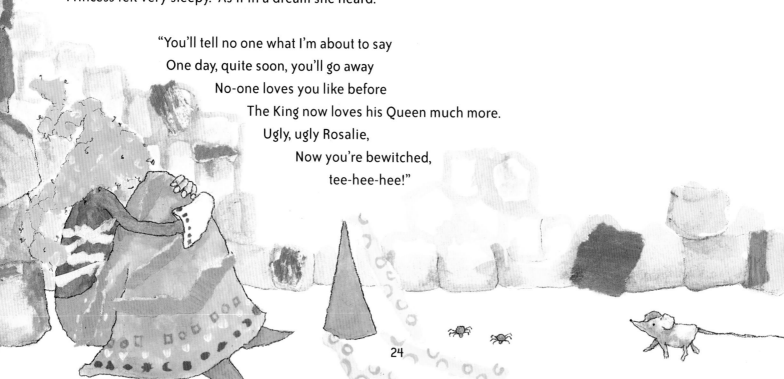

24

The Queen snapped her fingers.

In the mirror Rosalie saw a cross-eyed girl with a crooked nose, a puny little chin and straggly hair.

She got such a fright that she turned her face away.

And that's why the Princess didn't dare look in the mirror any more.

The next morning the Princess's bed was empty,
except for a little note.

"I'm where you can't find me. I know I'm ugly and nobody loves me.
Good-bye forever. Rosalie."

The King couldn't believe his eyes.

"Ugly....nobody loves her...where did she get that idea?"

He ordered his army out to search for the Princess. He promised
huge rewards, but nothing helped. Rosalie had vanished. For the
second time in his life the King nearly went mad with grief.

"Darling, how terrible for you, can I help?" asked the Queen.

She stroked his hair and whispered sweet words in his ear, but inside she was delighted, because one day the
King would forget about his daughter, and then she would be First Lady of the land.

If only the King had searched close by. Rosalie had left her room in the middle of the night, and traveled dark staircases and passages to a room high up in a far away tower where no one ever went.

And there she sat, all alone, until a little bird landed on the windowsill. "Chirp, chirp?"

"Go away," said the Princess sadly.

"Chirp, chirp?"

"GO AWAY!"

The little bird flapped off in alarm to his friend the parrot.

"Rosalie, my darling child, where are you?" wailed the King in despair. "Who can help me?" Suddenly he had an idea - the parrot!

"How stupid of me! Why didn't I think of him before? He's full of good advice."

The King ran to the room where the parrot had been locked up.

"And about time too!" screeched the parrot.

Looking rather ashamed, the King closed the door behind him. He put his hand to his mouth, expecting to sneeze. But nothing happened! He looked at the parrot in surprise.

"Silly King! Parrot allergy!" the parrot scoffed. "Ever heard of sneezing powder? That's what that witch sprinkled all over the place!"

"Sneezing powder? That witch? What are you talking about?"

"Your new queen!" squawked the parrot. "She's a witch!"

"How can you be so sure?" the King asked.

"It's something I knew right away."

"Why didn't you say so before?"

"I did! But you didn't listen!"

The King groaned and covered his face with his hands.

"Oh, how terrible."

"You can say that again." The parrot angrily turned the other way.

There was a long silence.

"Well," the parrot finally sighed, "will you listen to me this time?"

The King followed the parrot up the palace stairs, until they got to the top and pushed open the heavy door of the tower room.

"Rosalie!" the King cried out in a broken voice, and took Rosalie into his arms.

"You don't love me," she wept.

The King gently wiped away her tears and told her who her stepmother really was. But Rosalie didn't believe a word of it, for after all, she was still bewitched.

"Come with me," the King said resolutely.

"What's going on here?" cried the Queen, as the King burst into her room, Rosalie and the parrot at his side.

"Ugly witch!" snapped the parrot.

The Queen started. "Do be careful, darling, your allergy!"

The King exploded. "Get out of my sight! I never want to see you again!"

"Nyah nyah nyah nyah nyah nyah! He never wants to seeheehee you again!" the parrot taunted her.

The Queen tried to keep her temper, and said as sweetly as she could, "But dear, I love you!"

"You don't love me at all! You're a witch!"

Then the Queen dropped her act. Blazing with anger she screamed at the parrot, "You horrid creature! You sneaky bunch of feathers! It's all your fault!"

She ran, raving and cursing, around the room.

"Now, now, that won't do your looks much good!" squawked the parrot.

This made the Queen so terribly angry that she pulled out her hair and then jumped right out of her skin.

Rosalie and the King sprang back in terror, for in the twinkling of an eye the Queen had turned into the vicious, hump-backed witch she had been inside all along.

"I say, aren't you ugly!" laughed the parrot. In a burst of fury the witch lunged at him.

"Guards!" the King called out, pale with fright.

"Forget it! I can magic myself away!"

She flung her arms up in the air defiantly. But she was so angry her spell didn't work.
"Stumpy-stompy-dumpy...doop!" Nothing happened.
She stamped her foot in irritation. "Stump-stompy-dumpy...bloop!"
"Wrong one!" the parrot cackled.

The witch just stood there, stock still, stiff as a statue. For the parrot was right.
She had accidentally turned herself to stone!
Rosalie looked on, her eyes wide with horror. Her father too
was quite speechless. They stood there in silence until the little bird flew in through the window.

"Chirp, chirp!" he cheeped excitedly. He had a leaf in his beak with a big shiny raindrop on it. Carefully he laid
it on the ground in front of the Princess.
When Rosalie bent over she saw the reflection of a beautiful girl in the raindrop. Her face broke into a smile.
With a mischievous look in her eye she went over to the witch statue, and looked carefully all around it.
Then she giggled. "You're as ugly as you said I was!"
People say the witch was placed in the palace garden
and still stands there today. Viewing is free –
and now you can dare to say anything you
like to the ugly old witch!

My name is
Sparkle.

Make a real
princess's
crown.

Paste your
photograph
here

Thread a
bracelet out
of cotton balls.

Stick hair clips
through
cotton balls.

Make your own
skirt of
ice flowers.

Put on tights.

Wear ankle bands
made of
cotton balls.

Sparkle's ice skirt

What you need:
★ blue leotard or long-sleeved sweater
★ pink tights
★ white and/or pink crepe paper
★ about 3 feet of elastic or ribbon
★ scissors
★ stapler

Put on the leotard or sweater and the tights.
Cut out lots of strips of crepe paper (see picture).
Staple the strips of crepe paper onto the elastic or ribbon
and tie this around your waist.

Sparkle's ice jewelry

What you need:
★ cotton balls or a strip of gauze
★ glue or needle and cotton ★ glitter

If you don't have cotton balls, then make little balls from the strip of gauze. Then, to make the bracelet and necklace, thread the cotton balls together with needle and thread, or stick them together with glue. Sprinkle with glitter to finish them.

Sparkle's crown

What you need:
★ thick, gold-colored paper 16 inches by 8 inches
★ tape ★ stapler
★ scissors ★ two strips of material
★ cotton balls or a strip of gauze
★ hair clips

Cut the paper into a crown (see picture) and join the ends with tape.

Put the crown on your head and remember where your ears touch the sides. Attach a strip of material to each side with staples. Put the crown on your head once more and fasten the strips of material together under your chin, so the crown won't slip off your head.

You can also stick cotton balls onto hair clips and put them in your hair. This will give you a special ice hairdo.

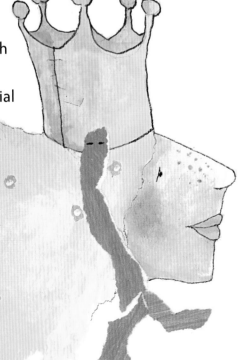

Sparkle's hand decorations

What you need:
★ red electrical tape
★ scissors
★ bits of red cardboard
★ tape

Cut red hearts out of the red sticky tape.
Stick them onto the palm of your hand, close to the bottom of your fingers.

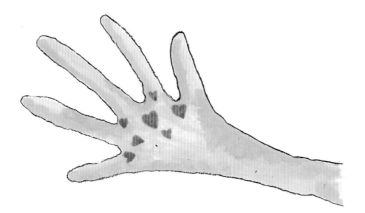

Cut out long nails from the red cardboard (see picture). Cut out a small piece of tape, fold it in half and stick the ends together. The tape should now be in a ring with the sticky side on the outside.
Stick one side onto your nail and press the cardboard nail firmly onto it.
This is a very tricky job, so ask a grown-up to help you.

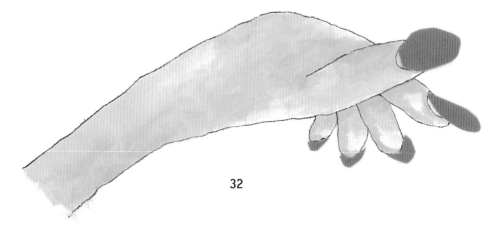

Princess Sparkle's customs

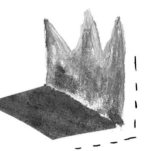

Ice princesses like Sparkle love playing among the ice floes. You can easily make these out of white or silver-colored cardboard (see picture). You can make them stand up if you fold them at the bottom.

An ice princess's favorite drink is lemonade with lots of ice cubes in it.

Sparkle dances with ribbons in her hand, because they look so nice whirling around in the air.

Sparkle

Way up north, in a country where the ice went on forever and snow covered the mountains, there lived a very special princess. Even when ice flowers covered the windows and the lake was frozen over, the Princess was never cold. Was that because her name was Sparkle? Or was it because of her hands? Her hands were always as warm as glowing coals. If you looked really closely at the palms of her hands you wouldn't see ordinary little lines, but tiny little hearts.

The northern country had no subjects because it was so cold and so far away. "Why are you King of such a cold and cheerless country?" his wife grumbled at the King one day. "I never get to see anybody."

"What can I do about it?" said her husband defiantly. "I'm not a magician."

"May I say something?" asked Sparkle.

"All right then, out with it," her father answered irritably.

"How about throwing a party? People love parties."

"What a good idea..." said the King in surprise. "Why didn't I think of that?"

Dear friend, I am having a party! Can you come?

To anybody who wants to come to a party

Sparkle could hardly wait for the party. Only ten days to go, she thought excitedly. She drew ten stars on her wall, and each evening she crossed one out.

The last night before the party she went to bed extra early, so morning would come more quickly, but she was so excited she couldn't fall asleep.

I know, she thought, I'll count stars.

Then I'll get nice and tired.

She pulled open the curtains. "One, two, three, four..."

In no time at all her eyes closed. Gently she slipped deep down into a dream. While she was dreaming of floating among the stars, a bewitchingly beautiful lady appeared in front of her.

"Hello dear Princess. I am the Star Fairy. Tomorrow at midnight, when the shower of a thousand stars rains down, you may make a wish. Make sure you don't forget."

Then she waved her magic wand and vanished from the dream.

The next morning Sparkle woke up with a smile on her face.

I think I know what I'll wish for, she thought.

That day a bitter wind raced across the ice. All the party guests arrived wearing thick coats, double-lined woolly caps, warm gloves and pale faces.

"Brrrrr!" they all cried.

"What does that mean, mum?" whispered Sparkle.

"They're all cold," her mother answered.

"Are they really?" Sparkle said in surprise.

Everybody shivered as they stood close together, and huddled deep down inside their coats.

No one said a word.

The King's wife nudged her husband. "This isn't much fun..." she whispered.

"Can't you do something?"

The King stood up and asked, "Do you know the one about the little polar bear?"

"No," shivered the guests.

"Listen then," beamed the King, who loved any opportunity to make a speech in front of lots of people. And he told a joke about a little polar bear.

The guests roared with laughter.

"And now we'll have some dancing!" cried the King.

Everyone stood up and danced in a long chain behind him - because dancing makes you lovely and warm!

The King enjoyed himself to no end. It's great to be King, he thought.

At midnight, when the party was still in full swing, Sparkle cried out in excitement, "Look, look!"

"Ooh..." a cry of wonder went up from the whole hall.

High above them hundreds of stars were falling from the sky, a sparkling shower of stars whizzing down without a sound.

"I wish, I wish..." Sparkle whispered fervently.

Secretly everybody did the same, even the King and Queen. When it had stopped raining down stars a great silence descended.

"Ahem," the King coughed.

No-one heard him. All eyes were turned dreamily towards the sky.

"Anybody for coffee?" he called out.

"Mm?" they all sighed absent-mindedly.

"Then off you all go to bed – there's room for you all!" ordered the King.

Sleepily everybody shuffled off.

Goodness me, he thought, it's easy to give orders!

The next morning, even before all the guests had left for home, Sparkle ran down the palace staircase and pulled open the heavy door.

"Oh, thank you fairy!" she cried, joyfully.

At the bottom of the steps was a little polar bear, sitting on a silver serving tray. Sparkle picked him up tenderly. Her hands glowed with warmth. The little polar bear snuggled against her and grunted happily.

"You'll always be my friend," Sparkle whispered.

"And you'll be mine," grunted the little polar bear.

Meanwhile, in a wild and wintry ice cave not too far away, the Grisly Ice Witch was shrieking:
"The Star Fairy, she brings luck,
But Grisly Witch, she breaks it up!
Grisly Witch turns heat to ice
All the animals, not once, but twice!"

"Mummy, mummy!" Sparkle was in tears as she ran through the front door. "We were playing outside and then suddenly my little polar bear was gone!"

"Well dear, I expect he was just playing hide-and-seek," her mother said, trying to comfort her.

"No, no, he vanished - poof - just like that!"

The Princess was inconsolable. She searched high and low, but the little bear had vanished into thin air.

"Star Fairy!" begged Sparkle, as she lay in bed that night, "I've got just one more wish. Please bring my little polar bear back."

The Star Fairy appeared and said, "Dear Princess, follow your heart and make your own wish come true."

Sparkle thought and thought. "If I have to follow my heart, then I'll go out and look for my little polar bear right away," she decided resolutely. Quick as lightning she got dressed and rode out into the night on her reindeer.

A heavy snow storm was raging. Her reindeer could hardly force his way through the snow and wind.

"Polar bear!" the Princess cried out in fear. Suddenly she heard a noise. The Princess looked around in alarm. "What's that?"

Sparkle couldn't believe her eyes when a frozen little ostrich popped up out of the snow.

"I say," Sparkle stammered. "Aren't you supposed to come from the other side of the world?"

"I'm looking for my friend," the ostrich shivered.

"The Star Fairy told me to follow my heart, but...it's so cccold here!"

"I've lost my friend too," Sparkle whispered sorrowfully. As she cradled the little bird in her warm hands, she told him all about the polar bear.

Meanwhile the snowstorm had died down, and the moon crept out from behind the clouds.

"Oh no it isn't! Oh yes it is!" Sparkle heard suddenly.

She looked up. Her mouth dropped open.

A motley gathering of animals were quarrelling in front of a signpost. It said: "Not to the Ice Witch".

"Are we supposed to follow this signpost or not?" the elephant trumpeted.

"I think so," snorted the hippo grumpily.

"Should we?" asked the giraffe doubtfully.

"I don't know, I don't know," squawked the chicken. The squirrel and the pelican couldn't keep quiet either.
"Whatever are you lot doing here?" Sparkle asked in astonishment, as she made her way over to them.
"You don't come from here."
The hippo was so upset he started to cry.
"We've lost our friends," he sobbed.
"And the Star Fairy said we had to go look
for them ourselves," said the elephant tearfully.
Sparkle was amazed. "Well I never...that's funny..."
"Very funny..." someone said from up in the air.
Everybody looked up in surprise. A snowy owl was
circling above them.

"That witch collects animals. Two of each
kind. But she won't get us!" the owl said,
laughing. "Follow me, we're nearly there!"
He flew around a couple of bends to the left
and then a couple of bends to the right. All the
animals were nervous as they followed him in a
line, until they couldn't go any further. A high, jagged ice mountain blocked their
way. An ice rabbit stood guard outside a hole in the side of the mountain. He looked as though he were frozen.
He didn't even blink his eyes. The owl just flew right past him into the mountain.
"How scary..." whispered Sparkle.

The owl turned around. "Not at all," he assured her. "Because there's something you can do that the witch can't."
Sparkle didn't understand what he meant. "What's that then?" she asked him curiously.
"You'll find out for yourself," the owl answered. Reluctantly Sparkle followed.
The hippo, the elephant and the giraffe looked anxiously at the little hole in the
mountain face.

"Will we be able to get through?" they wondered out loud.

"Take a deep breath and bend down," said the owl matter-of-factly.

They just managed to squeeze inside. The smaller animals giggled as they followed them into a maze of winding tunnels that led to the Ice Witch's cave, in the very heart of the mountain.

And there she stood, flashing her eyes and stirring a huge pot.

"Grislyfixy - animals the whole world wide - Grislyfixy loves you - so just you hop inside."

"Haven't you got enough?" cried the owl boldly, as he flew into the cave.

The witch looked up angrily. She scowled, her eyes like slits.

"What are you doing here?" she asked crossly.

Sparkle hid in fright behind the elephant's trunk.

Cool as a cucumber the owl flew over to a white curtain and pulled it open with his beak. A crowd of animals were huddled together, all frozen stiff behind a row of thick icicle bars.

"How dare you!" the witch screeched furiously at the owl.

Sparkle peeped cautiously around the elephant's trunk.

"Polar bear!" she cried, as she spied her little frozen friend. The witch turned in curiosity, to see where the voice came from.

"Ha! A human child, I haven't got one of those yet!" she cried in delight.

"Ikky-tikky-tees, everybody freeze!"

The elephant, the pelican, the squirrel, all the animals froze statue-still. All except Sparkle and the owl.

"Well I'll be blowed! Why don't you freeze up?" snapped the witch.

"You don't freeze wise old owls at the drop of a hat. That takes time," said the owl.

"We'll just see about that!" Cursing loudly, she threw up her arms.

Horrified, Sparkle crawled once more behind the elephant and held tightly onto his trunk.

"Tetteretetteretet!" he trumpeted as he de-frosted.

Startled, Sparkle jumped aside. "What?" she stammered.

"What's she doing?" the witch looked angrily at the owl.

"She can do something that you can't do," the owl answered triumphantly.

"Oh really? Pooh! Ikky-tikky-tees, everybody freeze! You're frozen." The witch tried once again. The elephant froze up on the spot. But nothing happened to Sparkle.

"Dash, dash and dash again!" The witch charged menacingly at Sparkle.

The Princess shrank back. "No!" she squealed and threw up her arms.

The witch froze in her footsteps.

"Ack!" she spluttered in disgust. "Hearts!" She stumbled backwards.

"Bravo!" cheered the owl. "Do you see what you can do?"

Dazed, Sparkle looked at her hands. They were glowing like coals.

"Oh, so that's the secret…" she whispered, as she saw the hearts sparkling in her hands.

She raised her hands up once more and held them in front of the witch's face.

"Ow, they're hot! It burns!"

The witch quickly turned her face away but her nose was already dripping. "Dash it!" She tried to run away but her feet were disappearing in little puddles of water.

"Go away!" screamed the witch. But Sparkle bravely stood her ground.

"What a dirty trick!" With a loud screech the witch melted away, until she was just a bubbling puddle on the ground.

"Now we must…" Sparkle whispered.

Hesitantly she took hold of the elephant's trunk once again.

"Tetteretetteretet!" he trumpeted right away.

"Yes!" cried the owl, "and now the rest!"

One by one Sparkle touched the other animals.

"Where is the witch, where is the witch?" squawked the chicken.

"I'll tell you in a minute!" Sparkle cried, as she ran to the icicle bars.

The moment she took hold of them, they melted like snow in the sun.

She hurried to the frozen animals. "Kangaroo, zebra, cockatoo, monkey."

42

Sparkle touched them one by one. They came to life at once. In no time at all the whole
group of animals were standing chattering happily together. In their midst
was the happiest of princesses with a little polar bear grunting
contentedly in her arms. When they all got outside, the ice rabbit was
still standing guard, stiff as a board.

"Hello rabbit," said Sparkle in a friendly voice. She stroked his head.

"So," he mumbled, blinking his eyes, "No witch?"

"No," the snowy owl grinned, "just a puddle of water…"

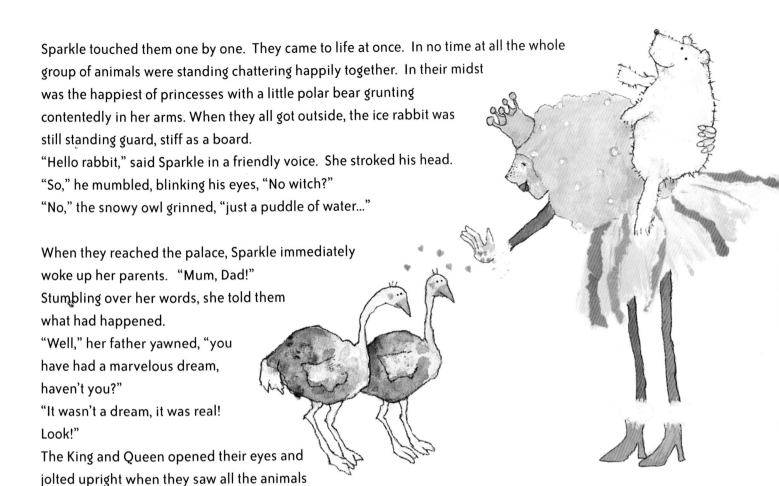

When they reached the palace, Sparkle immediately
woke up her parents. "Mum, Dad!"
Stumbling over her words, she told them
what had happened.

"Well," her father yawned, "you
have had a marvelous dream,
haven't you?"

"It wasn't a dream, it was real!
Look!"

The King and Queen opened their eyes and
jolted upright when they saw all the animals
standing in the doorway.

"Wow!" they cried. "This calls for a party!" the King said enthusiastically.

Hundreds of people came. The King acted the host beautifully and everyone danced once more in a long line
behind him. The next day the guests were still there, standing around in front of the palace.

"Actually, we don't want to leave. You give such great parties…"

"Stay and live here!" the King cried. "I'll throw a party every week!"

So everybody's wish was granted. For the King, a kingdom full of subjects to rule over and for the guests a country full of fun to live in. The Queen was delighted because someone came to visit every day. Sparkle's animal friends got to go back to their homes, where it wasn't so cold.

"Will you come back for a party now and then?" Sparkle asked.
"Of course we will!" they said.

So if you're ever way up north and you see ostriches, giraffes or elephants wandering around, then you'll know there's a party at the Ice Palace!

My name is Oceana.

Paste your photograph here.

Decorate your hair with ribbons or hair clips.

Wear as many bracelets as possible.

Pull up the hem of an old skirt and tie it around your waist with ribbon.

Drape pieces of colored material over the skirt.

Keep a few bracelets for your ankles

Oceana's dress

What you need:
★ a white undershirt or bathing suit
★ a grown-up's old skirt
★ narrow strips of material about 4 inches wide and
5 feet long or a couple of old scarves
★ safety pins ★ ribbon

What you also can use:
★ beads, buttons, dried beans or uncooked macaroni
★ bits of material or cotton balls ★ two potatoes
★ a knife ★ paint ★ scissors

Put on your undershirt or bathing suit. Put the skirt on. Pull the bottom of the skirt up to your waist and tie it with ribbon, so it looks as though you're wearing two skirts.

If you like you can now put the beads, dried beans, buttons and macaroni into the skirt, so that it makes lots of noise when you walk. Or else you can put the bits of material or the cotton balls inside, so that your skirt spreads out nice and wide.

Take the scarves or the long strips of material. You can decorate these if you like, but you don't have to. To do this, together with a grown-up, cut out a design in a potato. Dip the potato in paint and stamp it firmly onto the material (see picture). Let the paint dry before you go any further. You can also cut out pretty designs in the material.

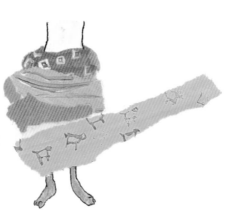

Drape the scarves or pieces of material horizontally around your skirt and then fasten them with safety pins. This is a bit tricky, so you may need some help.

Oceana's noisy bracelets and necklaces

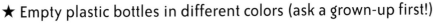

What you need:
★ Empty plastic bottles in different colors (ask a grown-up first!)
★ scissors ★ paper clips
★ three colored sheets of construction paper
★ ribbon ★ glue ★ beads
★ paint and a paint brush

Together with a grown-up, cut the plastic bottles into rings, so that you can make bracelets from them. Make the rings the same size, but you can cut them into different widths. Then you can paint them different colors if you want. You can also thread the bracelets onto a piece of ribbon, to make a necklace (see picture).

If you want another necklace, you can hook paper clips together. Stick little bits of colored paper to the paper clips to make your necklace even more colorful. You can also hang beads on the paper clips. You can make necklaces and/or bracelets from colored beads as well.

Oceana's hair

What you need:
★ 20 pieces of ribbon
★ little bows
★ hair clips

Make little bows out of 10 of the ribbons and fix them onto the hair clips. Put these in your hair. Fix the other ribbons into your hair with the hair clips. If you have short hair, this will make it look longer, and if you have long hair, then it will look even more like a princess's.

Princess Oceana's customs

African princesses like Oceana always find it a bit hot. To cool off they eat lots of fresh fruit. You can make a delicious fruit salad using lots of different colored fruits.

African music often has lots of drums, so make your own music using a drum. Or you can use an old saucepan and bang it softly with a wooden spoon.

Oceana

Once upon a time there was a princess who lived in a bamboo palace so deep in the jungle that she had never seen the sea. Her grandfather told her the most wonderful stories about it though, so in her thoughts she could see the waves and the magical colors of the water. The Princess couldn't understand why her brothers never listened to the stories.

"Who cares about stories..." said the Princes.

"Maybe you can learn something from them," said Grandfather. "Learning makes you clever."

"Pooh....we're clever already," the boys bragged. "We're brilliant at things like shooting arrows, throwing spears, and climbing trees."

Grandfather looked at them scornfully. "You do think a lot of yourselves, don't you? But you can't even look further than the trees, while your little sister knows all about what goes on out there. You'd better watch out, she's getting so clever, she'll be catching up to you before you know it."

One day there was a big party at the palace. It was the Princess's seventh birthday, which was a very special occasion indeed in this particular jungle, because when you turned seven, you were allowed to choose your own name. The Princess had been longing for her day to come. She'd known for ages what she wanted to be called.

The party was to be in the palace garden, but first the Princess was given a special bath of herbs.

"Mmm, lovely," she said, as she breathed in the sweet-scented perfume. "What is it, Mum?"

"Seven-years perfume," her mother explained. "It makes you strong."

After her bath, the Princess's skin was painted with lovely patterns and then she was dressed in special birthday clothes. When the Princess came out the royal elephants were ready and waiting. The Princess was allowed to sit on the biggest elephant of all. She felt very grown-up!

The elephants ambled along, in a stately fashion, past a row of dancing
birthday guests all singing at the tops of their voices, "Mamamamoewe!" to the
rhythm of the drum.

The Princess looked around her, radiant with joy. Gorgeous decora-
tions were hanging everywhere.

"Oh..." she whispered, when she saw a splendidly decorated
birthday chair standing in the garden. "For me?"

"For you," said the King. "A real princess's throne for you to sit on. Up
you go."

"Honored guests," said the King solemnly, after he had helped the
Princess onto her throne, "today is my daughter's seventh birthday. She
has reached the age when she is to be allowed to choose her own name!
Dear child, tell us, what are we to call you from now on?"

Expectantly, all eyes turned towards the Princess. She stood up straight, and said loud and clear,
"Oceana."

"Beautiful!" the King cried in surprise. He bent down to Oceana and whispered, "and easy to remember, too."
The Princes were standing so close by that they could hear what their father said. They were very cranky and
grumpy. When they were seven years old, they had given themselves really smart names. But the problem was
that nobody could remember them. After all, what kind of a name is Azibjakdoedamoemomowe? Or
Bowedjakomoepopotoe? Even the King and the Queen were at a loss, and decided just to call them A, B, C and D.
The Princes were furious! They'd thought up these smart names all for nothing!

"Oceana, what a silly name," they muttered jealously.

The King raised Oceana's arm and cried importantly, "Nobody shall ever forget, this child is to be called Oceana!"

"Mamamamoewe!" the guests sang, and then danced all the way over to the baskets full of birthday food.

"Oceana, what a splendid name," said Grandfather, as he lifted the Princess from the throne. "Come along with me!"

In a small clearing in the forest, just behind
the palace, something was hanging from
the branch of a tree, something which
Oceana had never seen before.

"What's that?" she asked curiously.

"A princess's swing. My friend the magician made it. You can feel the waves of the sea in it," Grandfather explained. He lifted Oceana onto the swing, and gave her a little push.

"Wheeee!" the Princess giggled, as she swung to and fro.

"Hold tight," said Grandfather, as he pushed a bit harder.

After that Oceana went on her swing everyday, and everyday she went higher and higher.

"Granddad?" she asked one day, "Can you swing so high you can see over the tree tops?"

"We'll have to ask the magician that," said Grandfather. "After all, he made it. And it's time you met him."

"Oh, how exciting!" Oceana cried. Hand in hand they walked into the jungle. They arrived at a simple little house, hidden deep in the forest. In the doorway sat an old man with pure white hair. A chain of bones and bird feathers hung around his thin, wrinkled neck. Oceana looked at him, but his pale eyes looked past her. Suddenly he said, "Welcome."

"I-I thought you couldn't see us," stammered the Princess.

"I may be blind, but I see everything," said the magician.

"How do you do that?" asked Oceana in surprise.

"I see everything in my thoughts," the magician answered.

In the middle of the house stood an enormous drum, which was so beautiful that the Princess couldn't take her eyes off it.

"This drum can answer the magician's questions," said Grandfather.

Oceana watched how the magician's wrinkled hands played the drum.

"Why do you want to see over the tree tops?" he asked.

"Because I want so badly to see what's on the other side," she sighed longingly. "Grandfather told me you can see how the sky touches the earth. And that there are seas and oceans..."

52

"How wonderful to meet a little girl from the jungle, who is
so curious about the world beyond the trees.
Many people don't even want to look that far,"
said the magician. "But if you know the
jungle, then you already know a bit about the
sea, did you know that?"

Oceana shook her head.
"Well, you know about tigers and snakes, don't
you? They can be wild and dangerous, but
sleepy and lazy too. The sea is just the same. One

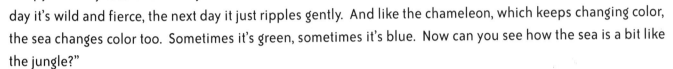

day it's wild and fierce, the next day it just ripples gently. And like the chameleon, which keeps changing color,
the sea changes color too. Sometimes it's green, sometimes it's blue. Now can you see how the sea is a bit like
the jungle?"
Oceana frowned.
"Yes, its difficult, I know," said the magician. "And I can well imagine that you'd like to see it for yourself. Ask
your brothers to push your swing. Because it's through them that you'll reach the world of your dreams."

Back at the bamboo palace, the Princess went at once to ask her brothers if they'd like to push her on her swing.
"Of course," they said manfully. "Good for our muscles."
But the Princess wanted to be pushed the next day too. And the day after that. Higher and higher - she couldn't
get enough of it!
"Oh no!" the boys sighed, when they heard Oceana calling again. They decided to push her so hard that she'd
never pester them again.
The Princes flexed their muscles and gave the swing one enormous walloping shove.
"Yeeaah!" cried the Princess and disappeared amongst the trees.
The brothers peered up into the air, their eyes narrowed into tiny slits.
"Oceana!" they shouted. "Ocea-aana..."
Finally the swing came back...but no Oceana! Thoroughly alarmed, the Princes climbed
right up into the tree tops, but as far as their eyes could see, no Princess...

They ran back to the palace to find their grandfather.

"O-Oceana's gone!" Stammering and stuttering, they told their story.

"Hadn't you better go and look for her?" Grandfather answered, without looking up.

"But where? We don't know where she is, do we?" spluttered C.

Their grandfather looked at them sternly. "I thought you were so clever?"

Then he relented and said, "There, there. I know someone who may be able to help."

"Who's that?" whispered D, when the old man appeared in the doorway of his house.

"That is the magician," said Grandfather. "He's blind, but he knows everything..."

The brothers looked at the magician suspiciously. A put up his hand. The old man did the same.

"He's not blind," said the boy. The magician smiled.

"When you put up your hand, you make the air move. I can feel that. Come on in."

The boys followed him reluctantly into the dimly-lit house.

As the magician made his way over to the drum, Grandfather said, "The drum shows him things no-one else can see."

The magician closed his eyes.

"So, boys, has your sister disappeared?"

"Y-yes," stammered B, in surprise.

The magician smiled. "She's beyond the trees, at the horizon. Wouldn't you like to go and see what it's like for yourselves?"

The boys trembled. They didn't want to go beyond the forest.

"The jungle's big enough for us," whispered A.

"Not if you want to find your sister..." said the magician. Gently he began to play the drum. The comforting sound made the boys sleepy.

All of a sudden an enchanting, velvety light rose from out of the drum. Everything around them went misty.

There was just the light and the deep voice of the magician, saying, "The sun goes down beyond the trees. So follow the sun, and you shall see..."

The magician fell silent and stopped playing. The light in the drum went out.

The boys looked in awe at the magician. But his pale eyes looked right past them.

Meanwhile, where was Oceana?

She had a terrible fright when she fell off her swing and flew through the air, narrowly missing the tree tops…she was falling! Then suddenly she felt something slide underneath her. She looked down, and to her amazement she saw that she was sitting on a glossy silken mat carried by butterflies. Oceana rubbed her eyes…was she dreaming? Carefully she peered over the edge of the mat. Beneath her she saw the jungle, like an enormous green blanket, and above her the clear blue sky, with little white clouds scattered here and there. And faraway, in the distance, the sky touched the earth.

The Princess looked around her in delight. How splendid it all was!

After a while the green blanket came to an end. Instead she saw an endless expanse of blue and green waves moving to and fro. Oceana felt her heart beat furiously. It must be the sea!

The butterflies descended gently and put Oceana down on the warm, white sand.

Then they flew away, without a sound.

Oceana stood there in bewilderment. She walked towards the surf and stepped into the sparkling water.

A moment later a wave gently picked her up.

With their hearts beating in fear, the Princes followed the sun. They pushed their way through the dense forest. They badly wanted to find their sister, but this was terrible! They got further and further away from their bamboo palace, until there was nothing they recognized any more.

"I'm scared…" D confessed.

A put an arm around his shoulders. "We'll b-be alright…."

For some time they had been hearing a strange, roaring noise, which was getting louder and louder. The boys started walking more and more slowly. Now they were in a forest full of palm trees, which had hard, sharp leaves. Meanwhile, the sun had disappeared behind the clouds. A angrily pushed aside a couple of low-hanging palm fronds.

"Stupid leaves!"

"What on earth...?" the brothers cried out. They froze with terror as enormous white monsters foaming at the mouth came thundering down towards them!

"Shoot them!" C screamed. The boys grabbed their bows and arrows, but to their horror, all the arrows went straight through the monsters!

Just as they were about to run for their lives, B screamed out, "Oh, look!" They had never seen anything so frightening in their lives…in the middle of the huge, foaming heads sat their little sister!

"Oceana! Hold on! We're coming to save you!" They threw their spears. Just at that moment the monsters let go of the Princess and she came sliding gracefully onto the white sand. "What are you doing here?" she cried. "M-monsters!" D squealed with fear, pointing behind her.

Oceana turned around and began to laugh. "Monsters? Those are waves! That's the sea, nitwit! Ha, ha, monsters!" The Princes started to go red. "The s-sea?

"Yes, isn't it fantastic! Just look at the horizon. Can you see the sun slipping from the sky into the sea? Amazing, isn't it?"

The boys looked at where Oceana was pointing, to the sun hanging just above the water like an enormous orange ball. They thought about the magician who had told them about the horizon...and about Grandfather who had said that Oceana would catch up to them one of these days. A looked jealously at his sister, who had jumped merrily back into the waves. He took a deep breath and said, "Come on, we're going out to join her." Followed reluctantly by his brothers, he waded into the sea.

Suddenly a wave lifted them up, and their feet were pulled from the sand. They floundered in panic. Another wave came, and then another. They hardly had time to catch their breath as they coughed and spluttered, tumbling up and down in the water.

"You're doing it all wrong!" Oceana cried. "This is how you do it!" She showed them how to play in the waves so that it wasn't scary.

The Princes went tumbling once more into the water, but now they found it much more fun.

When they arrived back at the bamboo palace, the children ran straight to their grandfather.

"Grandfather, Grandfather, we've been to the sea!"

They told him the whole story.

"Now that you've seen the world beyond the trees, you've felt the movement of the sea and seen the sky touch the earth. Isn't it fantastic?" said Grandfather.

B took out a big white shell. "For you," he said proudly.

Grandfather put the shell against his ear.

"You've brought me the sea!"

The children watched him curiously. He let them each listen in turn. To their amazement, they heard the murmuring of the sea...

The story of Oceana and her brothers went right through the jungle and in no time lines of people were standing in front of the palace. They all wanted to hear the sounds of the sea with their own ears.

Apparently people are still coming to the palace to listen to the shell.

So if you're ever in the jungle, and you see a line of people waiting, you might be very near...